Shake a Leg!

By Constance Allen
Illustrated by Tom Cooke

A GOLDEN BOOK • NEW YORK

Published by Golden Books Publishing Company, Inc.,
in conjunction with Children's Television Workshop

A portion of the money you pay for this book goes to Children's Television Workshop.
It is put right back into SESAME STREET and other CTW educational projects. Thanks for helping!

Is everybody ready?
Shake a leg!

Honk your nose!

Pat your head.

Waggle your fingers.

Wiggle your toes.

Rub your tummy.

Jiggle your ears.

Flap your elbows.

Shrug your shoulders.

Swing your arms.

Touch your ankles.

Knock your knees.

Kick up your heels.

Make a muscle!

Twist your waist.

Close your eyes.

Wave good-bye.